D0437166

This book is a work of fiction. Any references to historical events, real people, or real places are used fictitiously. Other names, characters, places, and events are products of the author's imagination, and any resemblance to actual events or places or persons, living or dead, is entirely coincidental.

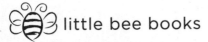 little bee books

An imprint of Bonnier Publishing USA
251 Park Avenue South, New York, NY 10010
Copyright © 2017 by Bonnier Publishing USA
All rights reserved, including the right of
reproduction in whole or in part in any form.
LITTLE BEE BOOKS is a registered trademark of Bonnier Publishing USA,
and associated colophon is a trademark of Bonnier Publishing USA.
Manufactured in the United States of America LB 0617
ISBN: 978-1-4998-0400-3 (hc)
First Edition 10 9 8 7 6 5 4 3 2 1
ISBN: 978-1-4998-0399-0 (pbk)
First Edition 10 9 8 7 6 5 4 3 2 1

Library of Congress Cataloging-in-Publication Data
is available upon request.

littlebeebooks.com
bonnierpublishingusa.com

Tales of
SASHA

Princess
Lessons

by Alexa Pearl
illustrated by Paco Sordo

little bee books

Contents

CHAPTER 1) Little Fairy Creatures

"Did you hear that?" Sasha lifted her ears.

"Hear what?" asked her better-than-best friend, Wyatt.

"A crunch from under this boysenberry bush." Sasha stepped forward to look. "Is it *them*?"

"Stay back!" cried Wyatt. "I'll look."

Sasha frowned. She should look first—not Wyatt. *She* was the brave one. Everyone knew that.

But everything had changed this week.

She wasn't a regular horse like Wyatt anymore. She was a flying horse—and flying horses were in danger.

"Sasha! You're home!" Poppy squealed and trotted toward her sister.

There were three sisters in Sasha's family. Sasha was the youngest, Zara was the oldest, and Poppy was in the middle. Poppy was the fancy sister. She wore flowers in her mane and tail.

Sasha nuzzled Poppy. She was happy to be home in Verdant Valley. So much had happened this week. First, Sasha had discovered that she had wings and could fly. Then, she'd gone away to search for other flying horses.

"What's he doing?" cried Poppy. Wyatt's head was buried in the bushes. Leaves and berries dropped to the ground.

"Searching for plant pixies," said Sasha.

"For *what?*" Poppy usually knew everything, but she had never heard of plant pixies.

"Plant pixies are little fairy creatures who live in plants," said Sasha.

"How cute!" exclaimed Poppy.

"Not so much." Wyatt lifted his head. "These pixies may be tiny, but they can hurt a flying horse."

"Can I see a plant pixie?" asked Poppy.

"They're not here. *He* made the noise," Wyatt said, pointing to a chipmunk. The chipmunk shrugged, then grabbed a berry.

"Happy days!" A purple horse cantered out of the shadows. The tiny braids in her tail twirled as she ran.

Poppy's brown eyes grew wide. She had never seen a purple horse! Her coat was chestnut-brown. Sasha was pale gray with a white patch on her back. All the horses in Verdant Valley were brown, white, black, or gray.

"Who are you?" Poppy asked.

"Kimani is my new friend. She lives in Crystal Cove with the other flying horses. She flies, too," said Sasha.

Kimani opened her wings. Her feathers were deep violet.

Poppy wasn't sure what was more amazing—that her little sister had found other horses with wings or that the flying horses were so beautiful.

Kimani inspected Poppy's mane and tail. "Wow! I never knew regular horses were so glamorous. Can you put pretty flowers in my mane, too?"

"Sure!" Poppy smiled. Sasha wouldn't stand still when Poppy tried to decorate her mane. She turned to Sasha. "I like your new friend."

"Here comes your mom and Caleb."
Wyatt pointed across the meadow.

Caleb, their teacher, was old and moved very slowly. Sasha knew it would be a while before they both reached her. She listened to Poppy and Kimani talk about using honeysuckle petals to make their manes smell nice.

"Boring!" Sasha spotted an apple on the ground. "Think fast!" she called to Wyatt.

She kicked the apple with her hoof. It sailed through the air toward him. Wyatt headed the apple back to her. She blocked it with one of her hind legs and knocked it back at him.

Then Wyatt kicked it too hard. The apple rolled under a large white mushroom nearby. Sasha bent to look for it.

A tiny, pointy face peered out at her from behind the mushroom.

A plant pixie!

A Real Princess?

"Whoa!" cried Sasha.

What should she do?

Wyatt had once sneezed on a plant pixie to make it go away.

Sasha tried to sneeze. No sneeze came out.

The plant pixie scampered off before she could try again.

Poppy giggled. "I can't believe you're scared of one little pixie."

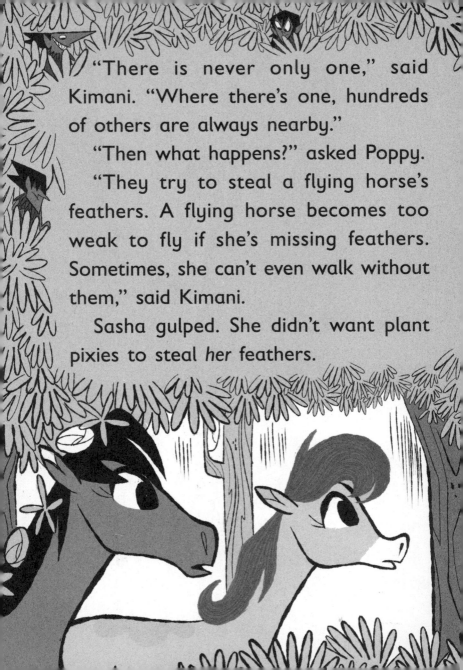

"There is never only one," said Kimani. "Where there's one, hundreds of others are always nearby."

"Then what happens?" asked Poppy.

"They try to steal a flying horse's feathers. A flying horse becomes too weak to fly if she's missing feathers. Sometimes, she can't even walk without them," said Kimani.

Sasha gulped. She didn't want plant pixies to steal *her* feathers.

"Wasn't a spell placed on Verdant Valley to keep plant pixies away?" asked Sasha. "Why are they here now?"

"The spell must have been broken when you went through the big trees," guessed Kimani.

Sasha had gone through the trees to visit Crystal Cove. No horse from the valley had ever crossed the big trees before.

Kimani searched the flowers and trees for other hidden pixies. "A lot will show up once they know the princess is here."

"Are *you* a princess, Kimani?" Poppy was excited. She'd never met a real princess.

"Not me," said Kimani. "Sasha is."

"Sasha?" Poppy asked in disbelief.

Sasha didn't act like a princess. She ran in the muddy fields with Wyatt. If anyone acted like a princess, it was Poppy.

"It's not fair," Poppy said with a pout. Caleb and their mother finally walked up to join them. "Sasha has wings, and now she's a princess, too."

Sasha blushed. She didn't want to be a flying horse princess—or *any* kind of princess.

Kimani explained that the flying horses had left Sasha in Verdant Valley when she was a baby to keep her safe from the plant pixies. "Sasha's feathers have extra-special power. If the plant pixies take them from her, she won't be able to rule the flying horses someday."

Caleb frowned. "Sasha can't stay here if she's in danger."

"Sasha must go back to Crystal Cove," her mother added. "The flying horses will keep her safe."

"That's a good plan," said Kimani. "Sapphire will know what to do."

Sapphire was the bright blue flying horse in charge of Crystal Cove.

"Can I come, too?" asked Poppy.

Kimani shook her head. "We need to go quickly. It's best if we fly, and—"

"—I don't have wings." Poppy sighed.

Sasha wished she could take her sister with her. She wanted to take Wyatt, Caleb, and her parents, too. She felt caught between the two worlds that she loved.

"I'll come back very soon, I promise." Sasha kissed everyone good-bye.

Sasha followed Kimani through the big trees.

Then the two horses flew up, up, up into the clouds.

The Princess Test

As Sasha and Kimani flew, the land below them grew more colorful. The ocean turned turquoise. The beach glittered with rubies, emeralds, and diamonds. A peacock on the ground joked with a spider monkey riding a scooter. Flamingoes played jump rope.

Sasha and Kimani landed on the beach of Crystal Cove. Horses of every color—red, orange, pink, green—opened their wings and cheered for Sasha's arrival.

"So weird." Sasha smiled and waved her tail. She never got this much attention back home.

"Greetings!" boomed the deep voice of a toucan. He was Sapphire's messenger. "Sapphire has been waiting for you."

He led them to a gold door in the side of a rocky cliff. The flying horses lived in caves along the cliffs. The door swung open. The toucan nudged her inside.

"Just me?" Sasha peered nervously into the darkness.

"I can't go," said Kimani. "I'm not part of the special meeting."

Spotting an amber light just ahead of her, Sasha slowly walked toward it. She entered a large room. Four horses in it studied a map.

"Join us, Sasha." Sapphire's voice was warm. "What's she doing here?" a large yellow horse asked.

"I want to help." Sasha had broken the spell. It was only right that she helped get rid of the plant pixies.

"No," snapped the yellow horse. "You aren't ready. You shouldn't be here."

"Now, Xanthos, be nice," Sapphire said to the yellow horse. She turned to Sasha. "Only members of the High Haras are allowed in here."

"What's the High Haras?" Sasha was very confused.

"The High Haras is this group. We rule Crystal Cove when the King and Queen aren't here," said Sapphire. "They're off helping a herd of flying horses on the other side of the world."

Just days ago, Sasha had thought she was the only horse that had wings. She had been so wrong! Flying horses lived all over the world.

Sapphire opened a wooden box. She lifted out a gold crown that twinkled with white diamonds and pink crystals.

"You are our Lost Princess, Sasha. Someday you will wear this crown. When you do, you will be part of the High Haras."

"That's *mine?*" Sasha reached out to touch the crown, but Sapphire quickly tucked it into the box.

"Yes, but not now. First, you must study this." She held up a pile of fabric.

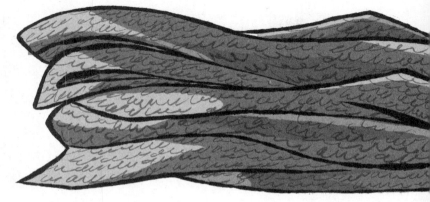

"Study a blanket?" asked Sasha.

"It's not a blanket." Sapphire stretched out the sheer fabric for Sasha to see. Tiny words covered every inch. "The story of the flying horses is written here."

"We sure have a long story!" Sasha joked.

"We do. You must learn the whole story and how to act like a princess to pass the Princess Test," said Sapphire.

"There's a test?" Sasha never did well on tests at school.

"Yes. Crimson will help you prepare." Sapphire pointed to the red horse next to her.

Sasha shook her head. "The crown is pretty, but I don't want to study for a princess test. I want to get rid of the plant pixies, so I can go home."

"You can only help if you pass the test," said Xanthos. "It's the rule."

"A princess has important hidden powers. We can't learn what yours are until you pass the test," said Sapphire. "We need your help. Only *your* princess powers can keep us safe."

Sasha knew she had no choice. She had to pass the Princess Test.

4) Very Princess-y

Princess lessons were hard.

Sasha spent the next day flying up, down, and all around. There were rules about how a princess should flap her wings (on a 1 . . . 2, 3 count), take off (no running start), and land (smoothly, of course).

Crimson said Sasha's takeoff was awkward. She said her landings were clumsy. Sasha did them over and over until she felt dizzy.

"Time to eat." Crimson spoke each word crisply. She was very proper.

"Bring on the food!" Sasha tied a white napkin around her neck. Crimson placed a carrot on a silver plate.

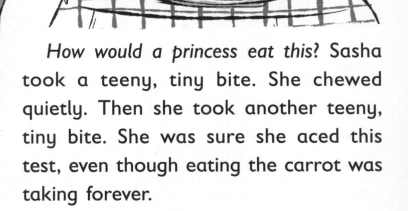

How would a princess eat this? Sasha took a teeny, tiny bite. She chewed quietly. Then she took another teeny, tiny bite. She was sure she aced this test, even though eating the carrot was taking forever.

"Wrong! All wrong!" cried Crimson.
"A princess should eat with gusto."

"What's gusto?" asked Sasha.

"Happiness and energy. Dig in, chew loudly, and show how much you enjoy it," said Crimson.

Sasha laughed. "That's how I always eat. I was trying to be princess-y."

Crimson led Sasha to a small pond where the water bubbled. "Try drinking now."

Sasha decided to drink the way she always did. She waded into the cool water. She lowered her head and lapped it up with her tongue. "How was that?"

"Not princess-y at all," said Crimson. "A princess never walks into the water she drinks. So gross! She gives a low curtsy, then sips."

"Seriously?" Sasha raised her eyebrows. "Okay, I'll try."

Sasha balanced on the edge of the lake. She bent her knees low. Her legs trembled as she tried to stay still. She titled her head toward the water and—*splash!*

Sasha tumbled face-first into the pond!

When she popped her head out of the water, her wet mane was plastered around her face.

Kimani was watching nearby. "You look ridiculous!" she said, laughing.

Sasha swam to the edge and shook her whole body, showering Kimani with droplets. "Now you're wet, too!"

The two wet friends burst into giggles.

Crimson didn't laugh. "Hmmm, princess lessons don't seem to be working today."

5) Triple-Tail-Twirl

"Thousands of years ago, more horses than birds flew in the sky," Sasha read aloud the next day.

She imagined the sky crowded with horses.

Crimson was making her read the story of the flying horses over and over. Crimson said she'd learn faster alone. Sasha hated being by herself.

"A horse's wing has many kinds of feathers. There are plumes, bristles, filaments. . . ." Sasha's voice trailed off.

She'd *never* remember these tricky names.

She couldn't focus. The words danced across the fabric. Her legs were restless.

Sasha wished she could be outside. *What's Wyatt doing back home?* she wondered. Was he climbing Mystic Mountain? Were Poppy and Zara splashing at the stream where all the horses drank?

"Hello, hello!"
The toucan poked
his colorful beak
into the cave.

"Finally! Tell me everything." Sasha
pulled him inside.

Sasha had sent the toucan back to
Verdant Valley.

He gave a report. There had been a
running race at school. Her oldest sister,
Zara, had written a new poem. Her
mother had found a field of wheatgrass
for dinner.

Sasha's heart
squeezed tightly
in her chest. She
missed everyone.
"Can I go back
for a quick visit?"

The toucan shook his head. "No. The plant pixies are still there, waiting in the flowers."

"They won't find me," said Sasha.

"It's too risky," said the toucan. "If you pass the test and get your princess powers, you can help get rid of the plant pixies. Then you can go home."

Sasha read the story of the flying horses again until the sun began to set.

"Am I ready?" she asked Crimson. She knew the names of twenty old kings and queens.

"Not yet," said Crimson. "It will take weeks to learn everything."

Weeks? No way! That was too long!

Kimani saw that Sasha was upset. "Sasha, you look like you need a break."

"You're the best!"
Sasha nuzzled her
new friend.

Kimani led her
to an enchanted
waterfall. Sasha
wished she could
tell Poppy about
the sparkly rainbow
water. Her fancy
sister would love it.

"Let's play hide-and-go-seek. Me first." Kimani darted behind a rock.

Sasha quickly spotted her braided tail sticking out.

"My turn." Sasha snuck behind the waterfall. The sky grew purple as night rolled in. Were her sisters telling bedtime stories back home?

As she waited for Kimani to find her, Sasha felt the white patch on her back begin to itch. She knew what the itch meant. Her body wanted to fly.

No, it *needed* to fly.

The feeling grew stronger and stronger.

"Found you!" cried Kimani.

"Can you keep a secret?" whispered Sasha.

"Sure," said Kimani.

"Triple-tail-twirl promise?"

"Triple-tail-twirl promise." Kimani twirled her tail three times.

Sasha took a deep breath. "I'm going to fly home. I just want to say hi. Don't tell, okay?"

Before Kimani could answer, Sasha soared into the sky.

Spotted in the Moonlight

Sasha flew under the clouds. Stars twinkled, and a full moon glowed. She began to hum. No more boring studying!

Suddenly, a green horse zoomed up on her right side.

Then another green horse zoomed up on her left side.

Whoosh! They threw two long, silver ribbons at her. One ribbon wrapped around one of her hind legs. The other ribbon wrapped around her nose. The horses held the ends of the ribbons with their mouths.

Sasha had been captured!

Together, the green horses gently pulled Sasha down to the Crystal Cove beach.

Sasha shook herself free. "What's going on?" she demanded.

"We're the Safety Patrol," said the taller green horse.

"We were ordered to bring you back," said the shorter green horse.

Sasha looked around. "Who ordered you?"

"I did." Kimani stepped forward out of the darkness.

"You?" Sasha blinked in surprise. "You triple-tail-twirl promised to keep my secret! I thought you were my friend."

"I *am* your friend. I broke my promise only because it's not safe for you to leave," said Kimani.

"We just got a report," called the short green horse. "Butterflies say the plant pixies saw Sasha out flying."

"Oh, no!" cried Kimani.

"Why didn't they see me flying yesterday?" asked Sasha.

"Plant pixies see best in the moonlight," said Kimani.

"As soon as the pixies saw Sasha up in the sky, the spell that kept them trapped in the woods and the flower fields lifted," said the short green horse. "They can now enter Crystal Cove."

"They will try to come for your feathers," Kimani warned Sasha.

Some flying horses nearby quickly ran to their caves.

"Where's everyone going?" asked Sasha.

"The pixies may try to take our feathers, too," said the tall green horse. "We need to hide."

"I feel horrible." Sasha's stomach twisted. She'd put all the flying horses in danger. She understood why Kimani broke her promise.

Sasha hurried to the gold door. She knocked.

No one answered.

She pounded as hard as she could.

The door creaked open. Xanthos poked his head out.

"The plant pixies are coming!" Sasha cried. "You need to let me help you!"

"Have you passed the Princess Test?" he asked.

"No," said Sasha.

"I can't let you in until you pass the test."

With that, he closed the door.

What Kind of Horse Are You?

Sasha raced back to Kimani's cave. She spread out the fabric history and tried to learn everything.

"I'm tired," Kimani said with a yawn.

"Not me." Then Sasha yawned, too.

Kimani fell asleep, but Sasha kept reading. Her eyelids grew heavy.

Sasha woke with a start. *Oh, no!* She'd fallen asleep—and she was using the fabric history as a blanket!

Kimani stood guard by the cave door. "The butterflies brought another report this morning. The plant pixies crossed over the mountains." Kimani tried to sound like everything was okay, but Sasha could tell she was scared.

The plant pixies would be here soon, and then what?

"Crimson is waiting for you," said Kimani.

"Ugh! Crimson is boring, and she teaches too slowly." Sasha followed Kimani out of the cave.

"Too bad you can't go to a princess school with a lot of fun teachers," joked Kimani.

"My princess school teachers would be Caleb and Poppy. Caleb knows fun ways to remember history, and Poppy was born knowing princess stuff." Sasha trotted across a meadow, then stopped. "Hey, I could really do that!"

"You can't go home," Kimani reminded her. "The plant pixies will spot you."

Sasha kicked at the grass. Her excitement faded. "Yeah, I know."

Was there some way to see Caleb and Poppy without the pixies seeing her? She needed a plan.

"Watch where you're walking!"

Sasha reared back in surprise.

The horse in front of her didn't have wings.

She didn't have a brightly colored coat.

She had black-and-white stripes!

"What kind of horse are you?" cried Sasha.

"I'm not a horse. I'm a zebra." She smiled. "We're different, you know."

"The zebras came from far away to visit us," said Kimani. "We're kind of like their cousins."

The zebra laughed. "Zebras are the wild and glamorous cousins."

Sasha stared at the group of zebras grazing nearby. She looked down at herself. Her pale gray coat was so plain . . . but maybe that was a good thing. She was getting an idea.

"If I've never seen a zebra, then I bet the plant pixies haven't either," Sasha said.

"So?" Kimani didn't understand.

"What if I disguise myself as a zebra? The plant pixies won't know it's me. I'll go to Verdant Valley. I'll get Caleb and Poppy to teach me everything so I can pass the test. With my powers unlocked, I can stop the plant pixies from taking our feathers." Sasha looked at her friend.

"That's a good plan," agreed Kimani, "but I'm scared the pixies will still see you."

"I'll be super-sneaky," said Sasha." "Will you help me?"

Kimani had sent the Safety Patrol after her the last time she'd tried to go home. What would she do this time?

Zebra-fied

"I'll help you," agreed Kimani. "You're our best shot at stopping the pixies. But how are you going to look like a zebra? You don't have stripes."

Sasha told her the plan. Kimani cantered away. A few minutes later, Kimani walked back with a small pot of black paint and a brush.

Kimani painted black stripes on Sasha's body. She copied the pattern of a nearby zebra.

"Do I look okay?" Sasha worried. "Zebras are black and white, not black and gray."

"You look like a zebra that needs a bubble bath." Kimani laughed.

Sasha stood in the sunlight so the paint would dry faster.

"Now it's your turn to be zebra-fied!" Sasha dipped the paintbrush into the pot. "Oh, no! There's not enough paint. Could you be a one-stripe zebra?"

"No one will be fooled by a one-striped *purple* zebra. You go without me," said Kimani. "Just don't let anyone see that you're you."

Kimani waved over the zebras. They were happy to help. The wild zebras liked adventure. Sasha squeezed into the middle of their striped pack. The zebras would walk to Verdant Valley—with Sasha hidden among them.

Sasha was nervous. Would her plan work?

First, the zebras walked past the peacock. He didn't spot Sasha.

At the lake, they got on the ferry. Sasha kept her head down. Would the beaver captain see her?

No! He was too busy steering the heavy raft of zebras.

Next, they began their journey, stepping into the field of neon flowers.

Sasha's heart beat wildly in her chest. Plant pixies slept in flowers.

"Stay close," whispered Sasha.

The zebras squeezed in tight. She smelled their warm, sour breath.

Rustle, rustle, crunch.

"What's that?" Sasha couldn't see past the zebra bodies around her.

Rustle, rustle, crunch.

Something was in the flowers! Did the plant pixies know she was here? Or did they think she was a zebra?

"Don't stop," warned the zebra on her left.

Sasha and the zebras hurried through the flowers. Then they walked through the big trees.

"We're home!" cried Sasha. She led the herd to her family's cottonwood tree. Her mother, Zara, and Poppy rested within its shade.

Poppy gasped. "Look! Striped horses!" The zebras rolled their eyes. "We're not striped horses. We're zebras!" they cried.

Sasha stepped out of the pack toward her. "They're related to us, Poppy. Like cousins."

Poppy reared back. "Who are you? How did you know my name?"

Sasha grinned. Her disguise had *really* worked!

Their mother smiled. "That's Sasha!"

Are You Ready?

Sasha thanked the zebras and showed them the best spot to graze.

Caleb studied the history upon the fabric that she'd brought with her. He and Zara acted out scenes of flying horses' ancient battles. Sasha liked seeing it play out in front of her. Slowly, the stories began to make sense.

Then Zara pretended to be the first flying horse to enter a cave at Crystal Cove. She stepped inside—and was surprised to find a giant snail. Caleb played the giant snail. The giant snail had loudly trumpeted a song of greeting, except Caleb could only neigh, and totally out of tune!

Sasha laughed. She'd remember the melody of the giant snail now.

The next day Poppy woke her before dawn.

She taught Sasha to canter with flowers in her mane so that the petals wouldn't fall out.

She also showed Sasha how to win a staring contest. A flying horse princess needed to be a champion at not blinking. Princesses had to keep total focus.

A flying horse princess also needed to hold in her giggles when tickled.

Poppy tried and tried, but Sasha couldn't stop giggling.

"I'll work on that tomorrow," promised Sasha.

That night Sasha got ready for bed under their cottonwood tree. Her mother and father walked back and forth on the lookout for plant pixies.

"You don't need to," she told them. "My disguise worked. They don't know I'm here."

"We want to be extra sure," said her father.

Sasha closed her eyes and fell asleep.

In the middle of the night, she felt a tiny poke in her side.

Sasha kept sleeping.

Another poke.

Was she dreaming?

Then a jab.

Her eyes opened wide. Had the plant pixies found her?

"Wake up!" It was the toucan. He poked her again with his beak.

"What are you doing here?" asked Sasha. It was still dark.

"The plant pixies are about to enter Crystal Cove," he said. "Are you ready to take the test?"

"Now?" Sasha's voice squeaked. "I don't know."

"Can you try?" he asked. "We need you right now."

"Of course!" She whispered good-bye to her parents. Then she and the toucan flew to Crystal Cove. They landed just as the sun rose. Kimani and Crimson greeted them. All the other flying horses were hiding.

"I'm glad you're back." Kimani hugged her.

"Me, too." Sasha turned to Crimson. "I'm ready."

"How?" Crimson shook her head. "You flew off, and I haven't been able to teach you."

"I've had other teachers," said Sasha. "They helped me learn in different ways."

"That's good." Crimson nodded. "Okay, let's begin."

Sasha pranced and flew. She ate and drank in a princess-y way. She won the staring contest. Flowers stayed in her mane when she ran. She remembered the ancient battles and the song of the giant snail.

"You passed the Princess Test!" said Crimson.

Sasha didn't believe it.

"What about the tickling?" Sasha blushed. "I can't hold in my giggles."

"No one can do that," said Crimson. "Not even me."

"Really? How could that be?" Crimson was so proper and serious.

Sasha gave her a tickle, and Crimson let out a stream of giggles!

"We took tickling off the test," said Crimson.

Sasha really had passed!

"Happy days!" cheered Kimani.

Sasha galloped to the gold door, which swung open as she raced toward it.

"Congratulations." Sapphire placed the crown on Sasha's head. Then she frowned. "You should not have gone away. We were worried."

"I'm sorry," said Sasha. "I needed special help to pass the test."

Sapphire nodded. "I'm glad it worked out. Now you can help us get rid of the plant pixies."

"I'm ready!" Sasha hurried into the cave. "Tell me everything. What amazing princess powers do I have?"

Read on for a sneak peek
from the fifth book in the
Tales of Sasha series!

Tales of SASHA

#5

The Plant Pixies

by Alexa Pearl

illustrated by Paco Sordo

Pixie in a Jar

"Let's talk pixie!" said Sasha.

The flying horses cheered for Sasha. She wore a gold crown. It twinkled with white diamonds and pink crystals. Sasha was the Lost Princess of the Flying Horses.

Sasha hadn't always been a princess. She also hadn't always been able to fly.

Sasha grew up in Verdant Valley. She thought she was a regular horse, like all the horses she knew.

Then one day, wings popped out. She could fly!

That was Surprise #1.

Sasha went to meet other flying horses that lived far away in Crystal Cove.

Then came Surprise #2. *She* was their Lost Princess. (Except now she wasn't lost anymore.)

Sasha had to pass a tricky test to get her crown. The flying horses said that passing the test would unlock royal powers.

"What else can I do?" asked Sasha.

She could fly. Could she also read minds? Change into a dolphin?

Four flying horses were having a

secret meeting in a cave. They were the leaders of Crystal Cove. Sapphire was a kind blue horse. Xanthos was a serious yellow horse. Crimson was a proper red horse. Mercury was a quiet turquoise horse.

"We don't know what else you can do," Sapphire told Sasha. "Your royal power is unique to you. It'll only appear when you need it most."

Sasha hated waiting—especially for good things like presents, birthdays, and royal powers. "I need it *now*. The plant pixies are on the move."

"Exactly!" Xanthos gave a loud

whinny in reply.

Six hummingbirds flew into the cave. The hummingbirds were the flying horses' helpers. They held open a large map of Crystal Cove in their beaks.

"The plant pixies are dancing here," Xanthos said, pointing to a jungle on the map.

"The plant pixies are skipping here." He pointed to some mountains.

"The plant pixies are twirling here." He pointed to a meadow.

"Soon, they will come here." He pointed to a beach.

Oh, no! Sasha gulped. The flying

horses lived in caves along the beach on the map.

"The plant pixies are coming to steal our wing feathers," said Crimson.

"We must stop them," said Sasha.

"It won't be easy." Xanthos brought her to a nearby shelf that held a large glass jar.

Sasha pressed her nose to the glass. A little fairy face stared back at her. A plant pixie!

The plant pixie had a pointy nose, pointy ears, and a pointy chin. Her skin was pale green, and her hair looked like soft dandelion fluff. Her dress was made with leaves.

"Her name is Collie." Xanthos pointed to a tiny necklace around her neck that spelled Collie in fancy script.

Collie sat cross-legged on a leaf at the bottom of the jar. A tiny tear trickled down her cheek.

"Oh, poor pixie," cried Sasha. "Why is Collie trapped in a jar? She looks so sweet."

Xanthos snorted. "Don't be fooled. Watch this."

He unlatched the lid from the jar. He slid a horse feather inside and touched Collie with its tip.

She startled and cried out.

Whoosh!

Thick vines sprouted from Collie's wrists. They grew and grew, twisting and climbing. They shot toward the top of the jar. Collie scampered up the vines like a rope. Her hazel eyes shone brightly. She was very near the top. Soon, she would be out of her glass prison.

The pixie was about to escape!